CHINESE MOTHER GOOSE RHYMES

CHINESE MOTHER GOOSE RHYMES

Selected and Edited by
Robert Wyndham
Pictures by Ed Young

For my brother Jim,
the best of big brothers.

Printed on recycled paper

Special contents of this edition copyright © 1968 by Robert Wyndham.
Illustrations © 1968 by Ed Young.
A PaperStar Book, published in 1998 by The Putnam & Grosset Group,
200 Madison Avenue, New York, NY 10016.
PaperStar Books is a registered trademark of The Putnam Berkley Group, Inc.
The PaperStar logo is a trademark of The Putnam Berkley Group, Inc.
Original hardcover edition published in 1968 by
The World Publishing Company. First Philomel edition published in 1982.
Published simultaneously in Canada. Printed in the United States of America.
Library of Congress Cataloging-in-Publication Data
Main entry under: Chinese Mother Goose Rhymes = (Ju tzu ko tíu)
Parallel titles in Chinese characters.
Summary: A collection of nursery rhymes translated from Chinese,
including ones on lady bugs, kites and bumps on the head.
Also includes the rhymes in Chinese characters.
1. Nursery rhymes, Chinese. (1. Nursery rhymes)
I. Wyndham, Robert, date.   II. Young, Ed, ill.   III. Title: Ju tzu ko tíu
PZ8.3.C443   1982   398.8   81-21030   AACR2
ISBN 0-698-11622-4
1   3   5   7   9   10   8   6   4   2

LIST OF FIRST LINES

The poems in this book are all traditional. Some have been translated especially for this collection. Others have been selected from one or the other of these two books:

Pekinese Rhymes, collected and edited with notes and translations by Baron Guido Vitale, published in 1896 by the Pei-T'and Press, Peking.

Chinese Mother Goose Rhymes, translated by Isaac Taylor Headland, published in 1900 by the Fleming H. Revell Company, Westwood, New Jersey.

AUTHOR'S NOTE

Every country has its nursery rhymes and ballads for children, and in the different languages they vary in style or detail. Yet children's poetry the world over is also amazingly alike in other respects and it is correct to speak of it as being universal.

There are the similar lullabies. There are the counting songs with three as the common denominator. Other counting rhymes which are for fun as well as instruction involve the fingers or toes. Universally, there are poems about animals, flowers, good and bad children, people who are tall, short, thin, or fat. So the reader of this book should find himself comfortably at home with the presentation in English of these Chinese nursery rhymes.

Of course no amount of scholarly knowledge can reproduce in English an exact equivalent of Chinese poetry because of the vast differences in the structures of the two languages. However, the basic human emotions, subjects, themes, and plots can be reasonably approximated in the writing transference. My versions in English are meant to convey the spirit, the feeling, and intent of the originals, yet render them freely enough to interest and entertain English-speaking readers and listeners. I hope this book will bring pleasure to every one of them.

—ROBERT WYNDHAM

Morristown, New Jersey, 1968

師傅騎馬沿街走我騎蛟龍水上游

太陽出來一點紅師傅騎馬我騎龍

As the sun came up, a ball of red,
I followed my friend wherever he led.
He thought his fast horse would leave me
    behind,
But I rode a dragon as swift as the wind!

高高山上一棵綠草有個吉吉它往上爬

我問吉吉你上那他說過了要吃蘇

On the top of a mountain
A grass blade was growing,
And up it a cricket was busily climbing.
I said to him, "Cricket,
Now where are you going?"
He answered me loudly, "I'm going out dining!"

露水吃飽了回頭就跑了

蟲蟲飛到南山吃露水

Lady bug, lady bug,
Fly away, do!
Fly to the mountain
To feed upon dew.

Feed upon dew
And when you are through,
Lady bug, lady bug,
Fly home again, do!

蝴蝶落我不要

蝴蝶飛我不追

Away floats the butterfly.
To keep it I would never try.

The butterfly's about to 'light;
I would not catch it if I might.

Flowers for sale!
Flowers for sale!
Come, buy my flowers
Before they grow stale!

This little fellow
A naughty trick did play
So they sent him to the melon patch,
Far, far away!

瓜地多草看的瓜熟了叫你才回去

你這孩子愛陶氣送你南窪去看

閒來無事叫嘎嘎不叫爸爸叫媽媽

河蟆、河蟆跳搭搭東洋大海有他家

Froggie, froggie.
Hoppity-hop!
When you get to the sea
You do not stop.

Plop!

He climbed up the candlestick,
The little mousie brown,
And he climbed up the candle—
But he couldn't get down.

He called for his grandma
But his grandma was downtown,
So he curled himself into a ball
And rolled himself right down.

前子兩把快子四雙

老張老張頭頂破筐

Old Mr. Chang, I've heard it said,
You wear a basket on your head;
You've two pairs of scissors to cut your meat,
And two pairs of chopsticks with which
    you eat.

What is it?

Turn the page to find out.

羅鍋子橋羅鍋子橋一蹬到比一蹬

兒高燈龍兒鬧草水皮兒深

銀魚兒咬着金魚兒尾大肚子

蝦蟆石上坐着哇兒瓜哇兒瓜的叫

If you chance to be crossing
The camel-back bridge,
Each step leads you higher
Till you come to the ridge.

The lantern grass floats
On the pond like a sail,
The silver fish bites
At the gold fish's tail.

The fat green frog,
Sitting there on a rock,
Croaks out his greeting,
"Warrah! Warrock!"

My boat is turned up at both ends;
All storms it meets it weathers.
On its body you'll find not a single board,
For it's covered all over with feathers.

Daily we fill it with rice;
It's admired by all whom we meet.
You will find not a crack in my boat,
But you'll find underneath it two feet!

What is it?

Turn the page to find out.

The answer

(a duck)

Little snail, little snail,
With your hard, stony bed,
First stick out your horns
And then stick out your head.

Your father and mother
Have brought some roast meat;
So come, little snail,
Please hurry and eat.

But where has that little snail gone,
Please do tell?
He's turned right around and
Gone back in his shell!

在那兒呢在墳頭兒後頭呢

的燒羊肉你不吃不給你留

出頭兒你爸你媽給你帶來

水牛兒水牛兒先出掎角後

一朵芙蓉頂上栽
錦衣不用剪刀裁
雖說不是英雄漢
一聲喊叫萬門開

A bright red flower he wears on his head;
His beautiful coat needs no thimble nor
> *thread;*
And though he's not fearsome, I'll have you
> *know*
Ten thousand doors open when he says so!

What is it?

Turn the page to find out.

鞭綜手臉
梅花腳
站着高
坐着倒比

What has feet like plum blossoms,
And a pudding-face sweet,
And is taller when sitting
Than when standing on its feet?

What is it?

Turn the page to find out.

The answer

(a rooster)

The answer

(a Pekingese dog)

Come and see!
Come and see!
A black hen has laid
A white egg for me!

要褲要掛天河吊角要褲要袄

天河打斜吃瓜吃茄天河劈分山

When the Milky Way you spy
Slanting stars across the sky,

The eggplant you may safely eat,
And all your friends to melons treat.

When it's divided toward the west
You'll need your trousers and your vest.

When like a horn you see it float
You'll need warm trousers and a coat!

It has eyes and a nose
But has not breathed since birth;
It cannot go to heaven
And will not stay on earth.

What is it?

Turn the page to find out.

上不了天下不了地

有鼻有眼不喘氣

The answer

(a dragon kite)

Two little sisters went walking one day,
Partly for exercise, partly for play.
They took with them kites which they wanted
  to fly,
One a big centipede, one a great butterfly.
Then up in a moment the kites floated high,
Like dragons that seemed to be touching
  the sky!

你媽穿着乍板鞋走一步踂拉拉十箇指頭露着三

小禿兒唎唎南邊打水是你爹你爹戴着紅纓帽

Dear little baby,
Don't you cry;
Your father's bringing water
From the brook near by.

A red-tasseled hat
He wears on his head.
Your mother's in the kitchen
Baking you some bread.

See, from mother's shoe tips
Peep three pretty toes!
Now baby's laughing,
There he goes!

乖乖寶貝兒你睡罷媽虎手來了找他

Willow leaves murmur, hua-la-la.
Sleep, precious baby, close to mama.
Hua-la-la, baby, smile in your sleep;
You'll have only sweet dreams
While my watch I keep.

楊樹葉兒嘩拉拉小孩兒睡覺找他媽

天皇皇地皇皇我家有個夜哭郎

過門君子念三遍一家睡到大天亮

The heaven is bright,
The earth is bright,
I have a baby who cries all night.

We keep a dog to guard the house;
A pig will make a feast or two;
We keep a cat to catch a mouse;
But what is the use of a girl like you?

養活豬吃口肉養活狗會看活

貓會拿耗子養活你這丫頭作甚麼

開門來看見他粉紅臉賽桃花小小腳兒一柄把櫻桃小口糯米銀牙

爬草根兩頭分路中來了小學生騎花馬拜丈人丈人夫母不在家推

As the sun rose over the mountain,
A student came riding along.
He sat on a dapple-gray pony,
And sang a scrap of a song.

To the home of his bride he was going,
And he hoped that she wouldn't be out;
He saw as he pushed the door open
The girl he was thinking about.

Her cheeks were as pink as a rosebud.
Her teeth were as white as a pearl.
Her lips were as red as a cherry.
Most truly a beautiful girl!

Beat the drum! Rum-pum-pum!
Here comes someone in a carriage chair!
Rum-pum-pay! Clear the way!
It's a bride who's riding to her wedding there.

Rum-pum-pum! Beat the drum!
The carriage chair is drawing near.
Beat the drums! Here it comes!
Now the way is clear.

新年來到糖瓜祭灶姑娘要花子要炮老

頭子要買新氈帽老婆子要吃大花糕

You'll find whenever the New Year comes
The Kitchen God will want some plums.
The girls will want some flowers new;
The boys will want firecrackers, too.
A new felt cap will please papa,
And a sugar cake for dear mama.

Bump, bump, please go away.
Don't let mother see you.
If she finds you there on her baby's head
She'll give me no money to buy my bread.

疤瘟疤瘟下去別叫奶奶看見

奶奶若看見不給我們飯錢

On the top of the hill,
By the road, on a stone,
On a big pile of rocks
Sat a bald-headed crone.

On her head were three hairs,
Which you see were quite thin,
In which she was trying
To fasten a pin.

She put it in once
And at once it fell out;
She put it in twice
And twice it fell out.

But the old woman said,
"I know what I'm about;
I'll not put it in—
Then it cannot fall out!"

這個人生來性兒急
清晨早起去
打集錯穿了綠布褲
倒騎了一頭驢

A hurrying man he always was,
From the day that he was born;
And to hurry to a fair one day
He rose at early morn,
Put on his wife's green trousers
To hurry to the sale,
Jumped on his little donkey
With his face toward its tail!

高高山上有一家十間房子九間塌老頭兒出來挂拐棍兒老

婆子出來就地兒擦看家的狗兒三條腿避鼠的貓短尾巴

On a very high mountain
A family dwell;
They once had ten rooms
But nine of them fell.

The poor old man walks
With a great deal of trouble;
His wife hobbles after,
Her body bent double.

Their three-legged dog
Is as thin as a rail,
And their rat-fearing cat
Is minus a tail.

Outside my door, I heard someone say,
A man bit a dog in a vicious way!
Such news I ne'er for a moment could stand,
So I lifted my door to open my hand;
I snatched up the dog with a slow double-quick
And tossed him with force at a very soft brick.
The brick—I'm afraid you will not understand—
I found in a moment had bitten my hand.
So I mounted a chair, on a horse I was borne,
While I blew on a drum and beat on a horn!

忽聽門外人咬狗拿起門來開開手拾起狗來打磚

頭又被磚頭咬了手騎着轎子撞了馬咬了鼓打喇叭

My little golden sister
Rides a golden horse so slow;
She'll have to use a golden whip
To make her slow horse go.

A little golden fish
In a golden bowl has she;
And a golden bird is singing
On a golden cherry tree.

A smiling golden Buddha
In a golden temple stands,
With a tiny golden baby
In his gentle golden hands.

樹金老鸛開了廟門金菩薩金手帶着金娃娃

小金垣騎金馬金馬金鞭打琉璃井金蝦蟆梧桐

高高山上一個牛尾巴長在屁股後。

四個蹄子分八辦腦袋長在脖子上。

There's a cow on the mountain,
The old saying goes;
At the end of her legs
Are four feet and eight toes.
Her tail hangs behind
At the end of her back,
And her head sticks out front
At the end of her neck.

這個小牛兒打滾兒這個小牛兒竟臥着我們打他

這個小牛兒吃草這個小牛兒吃料這個小牛兒喝水兒

This little cow eats grass,
This little cow eats hay,
This little cow drinks water,
This little cow runs away,
And this little cow does nothing
But lie down all the day.

老和尚背鼓來咯

The wolf has come,
The tiger has come,
The old priest follows,
Beating a drum.

狼來咯虎來咯

拉大鋸扯大鋸用木頭

盖房子給貝貝娶娘子

We push, we pull
To saw up the wood.
(We pull, we push)
We make a fine house.
(We push, we pull)
It has to be good
(We pull, we push)
To keep a sweet spouse.

(A Rocking Game)

So you be a roller
And roll with power,
And I'll be a millstone
And grind the flour.

(A Twirling Game)

Gee lee, gu lu, turn the cake,
Add some oil, the better to bake.

Gee lee, gu lu, now it's done;
Give a piece to everyone.

(A Turning Game)

你
追
我
我
追
你

喊
得
喊
喀
得
喀

A peacock feather
On a plum-tree limb,
You catch me
            and
                I'll
                    catch
                        him!

(Blind Man's Buff)

Up you go,
    Down you see,
Here's a turnip for you and me.
Here's a pitcher, we'll go to town.
Oh, what a pity! We've fallen down!
What do you see in the heavens bright?
I see the moon and the stars at night.
What do you see on the earth, so near?
I see a frog, and his voice I hear.
What is he saying there on the rock?
"Get up, get up! Warrah! Warrock!"

(A Lifting Game)